MARTY'S MONSTER

written by Nancy Ellen Hird
pictures by Valerie Damon

STANDARD PUBLISHING
Cincinnati, Ohio

The Standard Publishing Company, Cincinnati, Ohio
A division of Standex International Corporation
© 1993 by The Standard Publishing Company
All rights reserved.
Printed in the United States of America.
00 99 98 97 96 95 94 93   5 4 3 2 1

ISBN 0-7847-0098-2
Cataloging-in-Publication data available

Edited by Diane Stortz
Designed by Coleen Davis

CONTENTS

CHAPTER 1

Soccer practice was over.

Marty walked right past

her friend Robin.

"Marty, wait!" called Robin.

"We always walk home together."

Marty stopped.

"What a good practice," Robin said.

"That new girl can really kick."

"She is not so good," said Marty.

But Marty had a sick feeling

in her stomach.

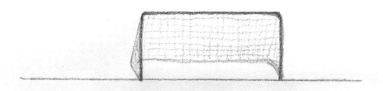

Marty looked back

at the soccer field.

That was when

she saw the monster.

He wasn't big

but he *was* ugly.

And he was slime green. Yuck!

"Look at that!" Marty said.

She pointed to the empty bleachers.

"I don't see anything," said Robin.

"In the bleachers," said Marty.

"You don't see a green monster

in the bleachers?"

"Monster?" asked Robin.

"What monster?"

Robin put her hands on her hips.

"Marty Milton," she said.

"You are not going to scare me

with some baby game."

And off she marched up the street.

"Robin, wait!" called Marty,

running after her.

But Robin was too far ahead.

Marty slowed down

and looked back.

The monster

was following her!

"Go away!"

Marty shouted.

She made her meanest face.

The monster did not move.

Marty turned

and quickly walked home.

Mom met her at the door.

Marty looked over her shoulder.

The monster was standing

on the sidewalk.

Marty scooted inside.

"Quick, Mom!" she said.

"Shut the door."

"Why?" asked Mom.

"Please," said Marty.

Mom gave Marty a strange look.

Then she shrugged and shut the door.

"Whew!" said Marty.

CHAPTER 2

Marty flopped into a kitchen chair.

"How was practice?" Mom asked.

She gave Marty a dish of yogurt.

"OK, I guess," said Marty.

"We got a new girl on the team.

Her name is Kris.

And boy, is she a creep!"

"Marty . . ." said Mom

with a frown on her face.

"OK, OK," said Marty.

"But she's not very nice."

"How do you know?" asked Mom.

"You just met her."

Marty poked her peach yogurt
with her spoon.

"Well," she said, "after practice,
I needed to talk to Coach.
But Kris kept talking to him.
And *talking* to him!"
Marty put down her spoon.

"Coach acted like

I wasn't even there," she said.

"Just because Kris

is a good kicker."

Marty got up and put her dish

in the sink.

Behind her, Marty heard

someone chewing.

She turned around.

There was the monster!

How did he get in here?

Marty wondered.

What is he eating?

And why is he following me?

"Marty, are you feeling

a bit jealous?" asked Mom.

The monster nodded.

"Me? No," said Marty.

"I have to practice now."

CHAPTER 3

In the backyard,

Marty dropped her soccer ball

onto the grass.

She looked at the goal

across the yard.

She kicked the ball.

Running after it,

she kicked

the ball again.

It shot into the goal net.

"Yes!" yelled Marty.

Marty picked

up the ball

and spun it around.

"Just wait

until the game

on Saturday,"

she said.

"Coach will see.

Everyone will see.

I am just as good as Kris.

In fact, I am better."

Someone smacked his lips.

I bet I am better as good as Kris.

Marty looked behind her.

Standing by the fence

was the monster.

He was eating again.

He was eating Marty's words!

He was grabbing them right

out of the air and eating them!

Marty stared.

How did the monster do that?

She put her hands

over her eyes.

But then she peeked.

Ugh! Was the monster

really getting bigger?

CHAPTER 4

On Saturday, Marty's team lost.

"Losing is hard," said Coach.

"But you all tried

and you played a good game."

Not me, thought Marty.

I did not play a good game.

I kicked the ball

out of bounds so many times.

I did not score once.

But Kris scored.

Kris scored our only goal.

Marty looked up

at the empty bleachers.

The green monster was there.

He waved at her.

Marty frowned.

Could this day get any worse?

"Oh, no," said Robin to Marty.

"Here comes my brother."

Robin's older brother, Josh,

socked Robin on the arm.

"Too bad about the game,"

he said.

"Maybe you will win

next time.

Kris is a great kicker.

Ask her to teach you, Marty."

Marty felt her face get hot.

She wanted to cry,

but *not* in front of Josh.

Marty walked away.

She could hear the monster

following her.

"Marty, wait!" called Robin.

Marty stopped.

She stared at her shoes.

"Don't listen to Josh," said Robin.

"You are a good kicker.

And you are my best friend."

Marty smiled.

Then Kris walked by

with Coach.

Marty stopped smiling.

"Kris thinks she is the queen

of the soccer field," said Marty.

She could hear the monster

chewing noisily again.

She put her hands over her ears

and ran to the car

where Mom was waiting.

CHAPTER 5

On Sunday after lunch, Marty
helped Mom load the dishwasher.
"We heard about Joseph
in Sunday school today," said Marty.

"I think his coat of many colors
must have been beautiful.
But his brothers
were so mean to him."
"They were jealous," said Mom.

"Jealous?" asked Marty.

She almost dropped a dish.

The monster laughed

and stuck out his tongue.

"Mom, have you ever been

jealous?" asked Marty.

"Sure," said Mom. "Most people are jealous sometimes."

"How do you feel when you are jealous?" asked Marty.

"When I am jealous,

I feel mad and sad," said Mom.

"Like someone

has taken my place.

"Sometimes I feel like

a monster is following me."

Marty's mouth fell open.

"Oh, Mom!" she said.

"Ever since Kris came,

I feel like a monster

is following me!

I wish Kris had never come.

Before she came, I was the best.

Kris is the best kicker now."

"But you are the *only*

Marty Milton," said Mom.

"God made only one of you.

And God wants to help you

be the very best *you*

there ever could be."

Mom put her hand gently

on Marty's shoulder.

"Marty, would you like to talk

to God about this?" she asked.

The monster yelled, "No, no!"

Marty looked at the monster.

Then she looked at Mom.

"Oh yes, yes!" Marty said.

"Please, let's pray."

She bowed her head.

CHAPTER 6

By the next soccer practice,

Marty had a plan.

The whistle blew.

"OK, that's it for today,"

said Coach. "Good practice."

Marty turned to Robin.

"I am going to ask her,"
said Marty. "Come with me."

Marty and Robin
walked over to Kris.
"Hey, Kris," said Marty.
"Robin is coming to my house
tomorrow to practice.
Do you want to come too?"

Kris smiled a big smile.

"Sure!" she said.

"Come with me to ask my mom."

The three girls
walked to Kris's car.
"We are going to have
a great team," said Robin.

Marty nodded.

She thought about the monster.

Was he still there?

She looked back at the bleachers
and grinned.

The monster was still there,
but he was smaller.

A *lot* smaller.

He was shrinking
even as she looked!